Jim Henson's™

DINOSAUR TRAIN™

Tiny Learns to Fish!

GROSSET & DUNLAP
Published by the Penguin Group
Penguin Group (USA) Inc., 375 Hudson Street, New York, New York 10014, USA
Penguin Group (Canada), 90 Eglinton Avenue East, Suite 700, Toronto, Ontario M4P 2Y3, Canada
(a division of Pearson Penguin Canada Inc.)
Penguin Books Ltd., 80 Strand, London WC2R 0RL, England
Penguin Group Ireland, 25 St. Stephen's Green, Dublin 2, Ireland
(a division of Penguin Books Ltd.)
Penguin Group (Australia), 250 Camberwell Road, Camberwell, Victoria 3124, Australia
(a division of Pearson Australia Group Pty. Ltd.)
Penguin Books India Pvt. Ltd., 11 Community Centre, Panchsheel Park, New Delhi—110 017, India
Penguin Group (NZ), 67 Apollo Drive, Rosedale, North Shore 0632, New Zealand
(a division of Pearson New Zealand Ltd.)
Penguin Books (South Africa) (Pty.) Ltd., 24 Sturdee Avenue,
Rosebank, Johannesburg 2196, South Africa

Penguin Books Ltd., Registered Offices: 80 Strand, London WC2R 0RL, England

http://pbskids.org/dinosaurtrain

ISBN 978-0-448-45605-8   10 9 8 7 6 5 4 3 2 1

Tiny Learns to Fish!

based on the television series created
by Craig Bartlett

Grosset & Dunlap
An Imprint of Penguin Group (USA) Inc.

Team Pteranodon is going to the Big
Pond today.

Dad is teaching them how to fish.

"I love fish!" Tiny shouts.
"It is my favorite food!"

"I hope I can catch a fish without a beak,"
Buddy says.

Dad puts his arm around Buddy.

"I know you can," he tells him. "You have great eyes and sharp teeth!"

Just then, the whistle on the Dinosaur Train toots.

"All aboard!" Mr. Conductor shouts.

Everyone finds their seats.
They wave good-bye to Mom.
"Have fun!" Mom calls.

The Dinosaur Train pulls up at Big
Pond Station.

Team Pteranodon gets off the train.

"Time to catch some fish," says Dad.

At the Big Pond, Dad tells everyone
what to do.

"First you fly out to where the fish are," Dad says.

"But, Dad, I have no wings," says Buddy. "What should I do?"

"We need a good spotter, Buddy. You can look for the fish from that rock," says Dad.

Dad flies over the water.

"I see some fish," Buddy says.

"Great job, Buddy!" says Dad.

Dad dives into the water and scoops up a fish.

"Ta-da!" he shouts.

"Now it is your turn, Shiny," Dad says.
"Try to be quiet. Loud noises scare
the fish."

"Here I go," Shiny yells.

"I am going to catch *so* many fish!"

Shiny dives and scoops up a fish.

"Me next! Me next!" Tiny calls.

She is excited to catch her first fish.

"Your turn, Don," Dad says.

"Here I go," says Don. "Ready, set, dive!"

Don dives and scoops up a fish.

"Me next! Me next!" Tiny calls again.
"I have been waiting for this for *so* long!"

"Here I go," says Tiny. "Dad, are you watching?"

Tiny dives down. But she does not scoop up a fish.

She dives again. But she misses again.

Tiny sits down and pouts.

She wishes she could catch a fish.

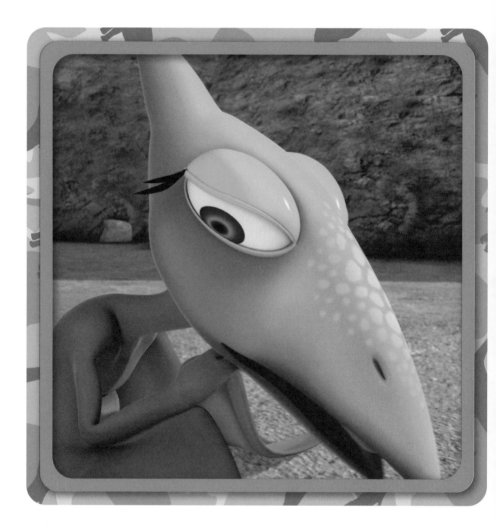

Dad puts his arm around her.

"You will get one soon. I missed on my first try, too," he says.

Tiny flies up to see Buddy.

"Buddy, I wish I could catch a fish," she says.

"Me too," says Buddy. "But I have no wings."

Tiny toots. Her toot scares the fish.

"I have a great idea," Buddy says.

Buddy climbs out to some rocks.

"You fly out and scare the fish with your toot," he tells Tiny.

"Then what?" says Tiny.

"When they swim to the shallow end, we grab them. You use your beak and I can use my teeth and arms."

"Get ready, Buddy," Tiny shouts.
Tiny toots and the fish swim to Buddy.
Buddy grabs a fish.

Tiny dives and scoops up a fish, too.

Shiny and Don cheer.

"Tiny caught a fish!" says Shiny.

"Buddy did, too," says Dad. "They worked together as a team!"

"These fish will be great for dinner," Dad says.
"Way to go, Team Pteranodon!"